The Dinosaur Who Stayed Indoors

Russell Punter

Illustrated by Andy Elkerton

Sid is riding on his bike.

He's off to visit Fred.

"Let's go cycling," Sid shouts out.

But Fred stares straight ahead.

"I'm watching **cartoon clips**," says Fred.
"Play soccer *now*? NO WAY!"

By Friday, Fred is feeling bored.

He sees his
friends online.

They're cycling...

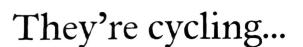

$swimming...$

playing games...

and having a
good time.

"Perhaps I'll join them," Fred decides.
"I've stayed in long enough."

But when he
plays a game
with Spike...

poor Fred's soon out of puff.

He tries a swim
with Dot instead.

They head down
to the shore.

But after just one
simple splash...

Fred's arms and
legs feel sore.

Perhaps a bike
ride will be fine?

But Fred's not
feeling strong.

He wibbles,
wobbles, then
falls off.

Oh no! It's all
gone wrong.

Fred decides to exercise – a little, every day.

And so he walks,
then jogs,

then *runs...*

until he
feels okay.

Soon he's fit to join his friends.

He runs down to the green.

"I'd like to play now," Fred declares.

Fred's really pleased to be outdoors.

But then they hear a cry of **"Help!"**
It's coming from the bay.

It's Molly, in a little boat.

She's drifting out to sea.

"My boat is leaking. I can't swim.
Please, someone...

Fred is first to
reach the beach.

He sprints across
the sand...

then dives into
the freezing sea...

and swims far
out from land.

Fred swims across to Molly's boat.

"Climb on my back," he roars.

He makes his way through crashing waves...
and takes her to the shore.

Fred's friends are waiting on the beach.

Now Molly's safe and dry.

They gather round to say well done.

"You're really brave,"
they cry.

But after this, what will Fred do?

Will he stay in once more?

Fred says, "NO WAY! I LOVE to be OUTDOORS!"

Edited by Lesley Sims